Spy of the First Person

Spy of the First Person

Sam Shepard

Alfred A. Knopf, New York

THIS IS A BORZOI BOOK PUBLISHED BY
ALFRED A. KNOPF

Copyright © 2017 by The Estate of Sam Shepard

All rights reserved. Published in the United States by
Alfred A. Knopf, a division of Penguin Random House LLC,
New York, and distributed in Canada by Random House of Canada,
a division of Penguin Random House Limited, Toronto.

www.aaknopf.com

Knopf, Borzoi Books, and the colophon are registered trademarks of
Penguin Random House LLC.

LCCN: 2017956676
ISBN: 978-0-525-52156-3 (hardcover);
978-0-525-52157-0 (ebook)

Jacket photograph: *Señor de los Pájaros* (Lord of the Birds), Nayarit,
Mexico, 1985 © Graciela Iturbide
Jacket design by Carol Devine Carson
Book design by Iris Weinstein

Manufactured in the United States of America

Published December 5, 2017
Second Printing, December 2017

In Memory of Sam

Sam's children, Hannah, Walker, and Jesse,
would like to recognize their father's life and work
and the tremendous effort he made
to complete his final book.

Spy of the First Person

1

Seen from a distance. That is, seeing from across the road, it's hard to tell how old he is because of the wraparound screen porch. Because of his wraparound shades. Purple. Lone Ranger. Masked bandit. I don't know what he's protecting. He's actually inside an enclosed screen porch with bugs buzzing, birds chirping, all kinds of summer things going on, on the outside—butterflies, wasps, etc.—but it's very hard to tell from this distance exactly how old he is. The baseball cap, the grimy jeans, the old vest. He's sitting in a rocking chair, as far as I can tell. A rocking chair that looks like it was lifted from a Cracker Barrel. In fact, it still has the broken security chain around one leg. I think from this distance it's red but it could be black, the rocker, some of these colors originate from the Marines, some of them from the Army, some from the Air Force, depends on the depth of one's patriotism, and he just rocks all day. That's all. Telling stories of one kind or another, little histories. Battle stories. People come by, and they see him sitting there on the porch in his rocker mumbling to himself. And they just walk up and sit down. They seem to know him somehow. At first they seem as though they don't, but then they do. Also there are other people who come by. Who come and go. One of them looks like it might be his son. Tall and lanky. One looks like it could be his daughter. Two of them look like they might be his sisters. They come and go from deep inside the house but it's very hard to tell from this distance how deep the house goes.

Robins are chirping approval. More or less. Robins are always chirping here, for some reason. I think mostly protecting nests. Protecting pale blue eggs. From crows and blackbirds. Swooping. Menacing birds trying to get their babies. Little robins with red breasts chirping madly trying to scare away the crows. Big bad birds.

2

They gave me all these tests. Way out in the middle of the desert. The painted desert. Land of the Apache. Land of the Saguaro. They gave me blood tests, of course. All kinds of blood tests testing my white corpuscles, testing my red corpuscles, testing one against the other. Then they tested my spinal column. They gave me a spinal tap even. They put me through MRIs. Tubes where they could look at my whole body to see if there was any paralysis in any bones or muscles. Cross-sections, sliced sections. X-rays. Ghostly pictures. And they looked at decay and they looked at all kinds of things and they couldn't come up with an answer until finally one guy, I think some kind of neurosurgeon, he had black hair and a white coat and glasses, electric probing shocks with a steel rod. He injected them into each arm and an electric current pulsed through and I could feel these shocks in my arms. He's the one who came up with the answer that something was wrong. And I said, well, I know something is wrong. Why do you think I'm in here? He just looked at me with a blank stare.

In the mornings I would have breakfast at a Mexican joint. Enchiladas. Cheese and eggs. Green chili.

3

There used to be orchards as far as the eye could see. Like picture postcards. Orange orchards, olive orchards, grape orchards, avocado orchards, lemon orchards, pear orchards. Orchards of every kind corresponding to the nationality that brought them here. For instance, the Italians and the Spanish brought oranges, avocados—well, the avocados came up through Mexico—tangerines, grapefruit, those kinds of things. The Italians brought olives. Out through Padua, sweeping silver leaves, limbs gnarled like old sailors. Black bark, silvery leaves. There were oceans of olive orchards everywhere. Way up in Chico there were almond orchards. Almond orchards that turned white in spring. Beautiful almond orchards that looked like Japanese calligraphy. Gorgeous. Walnut groves. Palm trees out in the Indio desert. Tall. Really tall. Some of them 100 feet or more. There was a border town between California and Arizona. The Colorado River ran through it. It was 1953 and white men used to dress up as Arabs on camels and parade back and forth in the street wearing Shriner caps pretending to be full of Arab pride. They were guys from the Midwest who owned barber shops and drugstores and had thick glasses. They had never seen the desert. I used to ride in the back seat of a Chrysler, right past the Colorado River with my aunt, my great-aunt who had blue hair and she was Welsh and her husband was fairly wealthy, but he had died by that time. His name was Charlie Upton, from Liverpool. And he had a penchant for whiskey and barroom brawls. In one of these fights he had his ear bitten off. Mike Tyson style. Bit right in half so that he only had one half an ear on one side of his face. I forget which side that was. But anyhow, he was wealthy enough to buy a Chrysler sedan on the black market during the War. Big heavy car. Beautiful car. Good for the open road. It had plaid seats. Plaid, not any other color but red plaid. I was all alone in a sea of plaid. It had an armrest that folded down in the middle of the back seat and behind each of the front seats was a kind of cord that went across, I suppose to support yourself for getting in and out of the vehicle if you were old. I wasn't that old then, maybe eight or nine, and my great-aunt who was my mother's mother's sister, her name was Grace and she had blue hair. She would drive me out there to Indio to the date festival where we would get date shakes and watch the white men pretend to be Arabs on camels parading back and forth in the heat. From the tops of the 100-foot palm trees you could see parrots peeking out. Red. Black. And green. Date shakes, imagine that.

There's a place along the way that always made me feel peaceful and I don't know why. There's a wharf behind it. The wharf leads out to the Pacific. The wharf creaks and moans. Sometimes it chatters and thuds when cars cross it. The timbers rattle. Sand covers the sidewalk. Sand blown in from the beach. Surfers twelve years old or maybe thirteen carry their boards under their arms coming home in the twilight. Bermuda shorts on, hair all oily, covered in sand. Small dogs walk behind them. Small dogs of no significant breed. Pelicans cling to the wharf. Seagulls swoop. Sandpipers hum and sing and dance their little dance. The seaweed is soaking. Far in the distance two people are getting up from the beach just in bathing suits folding a huge orange towel. The squirrels are scurrying for cover. The sun is setting on the Pacific. People are unlocking their cars from a distance. Pushing buttons, zapping their cars, making the doors buzz and sing, making little *Close Encounters of the Third Kind* noises. People are getting in and starting their cars, driving out of the parking lot under the palm trees, past the lawns, past the glassed-in sitting rooms where blond women are serving them lobster. Somebody is turning off a lawn mower. Somebody's sitting at a bus stop. Somebody's waiting for somebody. Lights are coming on. They're starting to serve dinner. They're bringing steaming pots of something. Something like crab. Something like cod. Bowls full of cod. Bowls full of hot rice. People are going home. Somebody is waiting for somebody. Somebody's waiting for a bus. Everybody's waiting for somebody to take them out of there—to take them far away. Down below they're just starting to swim and it's not even really dark yet but they are starting. Old men starting to drink. Young women are smoking cigarettes. The boats are rocking back and forth, back and forth. Bells are chiming. Some boats are unloading nets. Nets full of octopus spilling on the wharf. Somebody's waiting.

But inside this room they're laying down plates full of oyster, plates full of lobster. Steaming fish and rice. They're pouring huge glasses full of beer.

Moving toward the windows, someone comments on the race. I do remember this. Someone says, "A horse has been shot. The leader. The lead horse has been shot. A jockey is down on the ground. There goes the morning line."

4

I'm not normally a suspicious person. I don't go around looking over my shoulder for surprises. But I have the sense—I can't help having the sense—that someone is watching me. Someone wants to know something. Someone wants to know something about me that I don't even know myself. I can feel him getting closer and closer. I can hear breathing. I can tell he's male by the smell of his breath. I don't know what he wants. He gets more and more curious about my comings and goings. About me. He seems to want to know something about my origins.

5

Where exactly do we come from? That's one question. Was it a desert? Was it a forest? Was it a mountain? Was it the prairie? Where do we actually come from? The Colorado River?

If you were traveling in a foreign country and you lost your dogs and you lost your car and you lost your note from home that your mother pinned on your collar and you lost your clothes and you were standing there naked and somebody came up to you and said, where do you belong, how would you answer? Would you ask the one ancestor who happened to be Portuguese? Or would you ask the Spanish Armada? Somebody has forgotten.

6

To tell you the truth, I don't know where he came from. I discovered him quite by accident. Bent backwards, gasping for air. One day I was sitting here much the same way as he's sitting now, twiddling my thumbs, and I was looking out across the road and I saw this chair rocking back and forth and then I saw that somebody was in it. And there he was. He just appeared. I don't know whether he rented or bought the house and then invited his people there or whether they were already there and he came to visit them or whether he's on a short-term lease. I don't know exactly. Sometimes people appear like that out of nowhere. They just appear and then they disappear. Very fast. Just like a photograph that emerges from a chemical bath.

7

I'm not sure what he's seeing now, the air is so hazy, I'm not sure what I'm seeing either. Whether he's talking to himself or talking to someone else or what exactly he's doing. The birds are not singing now. Fluffy white clouds all around but the air is still hazy. The trees are coming back to life. A pair of old red tennis shoes dangles from the telephone wires, hanging up there by shredded laces.

He eats cheese and crackers all day. Iced tea. He sips on that. But he has particular trouble with his hands and arms, I've noticed. His hands and arms don't work much. He uses his legs, his knees, his thighs, to bring his arms and hands to his face in order to be able to eat his cheese and crackers. It seems that periodically he has to go to the bathroom or something. He stands. He wavers when he stands. He looks like he's going to fall over. Topple. It must be the reason for the handicapped sign hanging from the rearview mir-

ror of his car in the driveway. He wavers from side
to side. He signals. He looks like he might very
well fall over, but he doesn't. Sometimes he calls
for one of his people—one of his sons or daugh-
ters or somebody else closely related to him like
his sisters. He signals and they come out on the
porch. In other words, he stands, he wavers, he
does these things over and over again. Cheese and
crackers, iced tea, reading. Then he calls somebody and they come and they tend to him. They
take him inside the house. They take him by the
arm and take him inside. He goes through a screen
door into a dark house and disappears. There's no
telling how deep the house goes. When he comes
back, often with the same person, arm in arm,
they either zip him up or zip him down. They zip
up his pants. In other words he's done something
very private. He's either urinated or gone number
two and they help him with this. They help put
him back together and then they stick him back
in his rocking chair. They sort of gently lower
him back down even though at a certain point
he kind of falls into the chair backwards panting
and gasping. He says, the more helpless I get, the
more remote I become. Am I seeing all of this?
The air is still hazy. You might ask yourself why.

Why am I so interested. Is it pure curiosity or do I have some other motive. For instance, hired by some cryptic detective agency. Or is everything by accident?

8

Why is he watching me? I can't understand that. Nothing seems to be working now. Hands. Arms. Legs. Nothing. I just lie here. Waiting for someone to find me. I just look up at the sky. I can smell him close by.

9

It was that time of day that I love so much. That people have written songs about. The time of day when afternoon is turning to night. Twilight, I guess it's called, and I snuck across the road. I snuck across the road hoping to get a peek at him before he began any conversation with somebody unseen or seen. I crossed the road. It had been raining for three days straight. Raining. The street was still running with water. Water was coming down everywhere. Not rain but residual water. I got to the other side through the parked cars, through all kinds of parked cars. There were Toyotas, there were Chevys, there were Fords, there were Zumbayas. All kinds of cars and I got to the hedge which was neither a camellia hedge or a hydrangea or anything like that. It was unidentifiable. There were white flowers coming out of it but I didn't know quite what they were. I can make him out through the white flowers, through the hedge. But I wasn't quite sure. I could make something out through there, but I wasn't sure what. Oh never mind, I'll figure it out later. That's the thing about later. You don't know what's coming up. You don't know how all the loose ends are going to gather together. Something for sure is going to happen but you don't know what it is. For instance—I'm outside, for instance. Out here with the birds and the bugs. Not exactly outside, but close enough. Just across the way. It's never like it was. The clouds. The big sky. The flowers. The chirping.

10

It seems like only yesterday we were playing bocce. You and me. You were a man by that time. Bocce was an old man's sport but you were a young man. You liked the weight of the iron ball, hitting the sand with a thud. Hitting each other with a clunk. We set our coffee on the handrail. We were playing in an old restaurant. They had a sand court in there. An old restaurant that used to be a granary. Or a prune warehouse. I forget which. In a small town way up north. Half inside and half outside. They made it seem very Italian. Very Old World. The hanging light bulbs. Different colors. The brick walls. Dripping candle wax. In a small town where migrant workers stand on corners looking for work. Sitting at bus stops for a bus that never comes. Who don't seem to care one way or the other whether they get work. They just get together every morning for the camaraderie. The conversation. All these migrant workers speaking their own language. Just for the sake of making contact with the known. I feel very clear about all this now. It's as though I can see it. There is, as I remember, a coffee shop run by a young woman from Berkeley. She made lots of coffee in there. All types. Some from Brazil. Africa. Deep in the heart of old Mexico. You were having some sort of affair with her. Back then when it seemed like only yesterday. I slept on your laundry room floor. Blue cement. All night long I listened to cars going back and forth to Calistoga. I guess it was Calistoga. Where else would they go? People on vacation. People with nothing better to do. You slept in the loft you built. You had a Manx cat. You had a tailless big Manx. It used to jump from its ceiling perch down to your sleeping bag and throttle you by the neck. It was fawn colored and had tufts on its ears. I think his name was Max. And you later went to work at a feed store. You were a specialist in canaries, I think. You knew all their songs. You knew where each one came from by its song. Italy, England, Spain, Turkey, Greece, France. Each one unique. All day long you were gone collecting songs. You were a collector. Eggs. Colors. Some bright yellow. Some bright orange. Some muted. There was one black one. A black canary. Without a song.

11

I can't help feeling a similarity between him and me. I don't know what it is. Sometimes it feels like we're the same person. A lost twin. The eyebrows. The chin. The twitch of an ear. The hands in pockets. The way the eyes look confident and lost at the same time.

12

You were always getting up quite early back then. Way before me. Six or five something like that. Feeding Max something smelly. I heard the can hit the trash. I still hear the can hit the trash. You were always going off to work in your feed store with your canaries in another town not too far from here. Another small town of its own. This country was full of small towns back then. You were also working with chickens, as I remember. Speckled chickens. Leghorns. Layers of white eggs. I remember some kind of Spanish chicken. A very unique color to their egg. Not white at all. The egg was blue as the sky. Sometimes the slightest shade of green. I used to watch them in our little chicken coop back home. I would sit under the shade of an old avocado tree. It was so old that it drooped to the ground. Some of the branches had gone right into the ground and rooted themselves. A gigantic tree. The chickens loved it. It provided them with lots of shade and they could hear coyotes coming because a coyote would always crunch the dry leaves. Anyway, the time I am referring to is the time when you were living in that garage in a little house. Living in a garage in a very small town in northern California where the migrant workers stand on corners looking for work or hoping to get some. Usually pruning, raking, working in orchards. Pruning grapes. Gathering the leftovers. They would burn all that stuff in the middle of the fields. Smoky cones drifting out to the freeway.

Right now there's a gigantic plume, a white cloud, raising its head above the farm. My daughter says it looks like an atom bomb. She's very smart that way. She sees things. She sees things before they happen.

13

Back then you had all these stones in the yard. Do you remember? Red, green, blue, white, gray, all different colors. Very clear. Stones. You had something in mind. Shapes. Figures. You were working on them. Different stones. You were working on them with hand tools, chisels, hammers and rasps. There was one really fragile one, a green figure, that you were afraid you might break the neck off of. Stone. You had to be very careful how you struck it because one false move and the head would be at your feet. I remember your hands. Your hands in relation to the stone. Very clear. A backyard with a chain link fence around it. There was water somewhere, a water fountain. You went to Berkeley or Oakland in your truck. You went to find a stone and you liked this one particular place. This quarry. Because the man, a little Italian guy who ran it, seemed to know something about stone and he always guided you in the right direction. There were all these fires around, fires dotted the landscape, it was the season of fires. We were having sandwiches somewhere behind a picture window and I think we'd gone swimming at Indian Springs in the hot spring water up there with palm trees all around and snakes. The water was so hot when it came out of the mountain that it would steam. Huge steam clouds reached up to the sky. It would have to cool down in one pond before it got into another because it was way too hot to swim in. I remember that very clearly.

You finished the sculpture, the green one. Stone. You finished it and put it in the kitchen above that old black-and-white television set.

14

Sometimes, very often, he speaks to himself. Who else could it be? I see from this distance—I see that his lips are moving. His lips are keeping him company. But it's very hard to tell. His gestures—well, his gestures are the same, as if he's talking to someone else. There must be someone else. But it's very hard to tell. Sometimes.

Sometimes something sweeps across me. I'm not sure what it is. Sometimes swooping like the wind. Sometimes toenails or just the toes in the surf. Sometimes color. I remember sometimes you would start whole stories. Sometimes paragraphs. Sometimes sentences with the word "sometimes." Do you remember how you did that? I thought it was a good way to start. "Sometimes." In other words not always but sometimes. In other words sometimes not always. Sometimes this or that. Sometimes birds. Why birds, you would say. Why birds? Sometimes. Why color? Sometimes. Why . . . wind? Dogs? Sometimes it made complete sense to me. It made complete sense.

Or you would start a sentence or a story with "for instance." For instance, a single oak tree growing. For instance, the wind comes. The leaves fall. The dog pants. The flies buzz. The butterflies go in and out. The leaves fall for instance sometimes not all the sometime. Just sometimes.

I think sometimes there's something wrong with him, actually. People attend to him sometimes and sometimes he just sits there alone talking to himself. No gestures at all. Or he falls asleep. Sometimes I wish I were back in that time. There's a car in the driveway with a blue handicapped sticker. A white car. A white car with an Arizona plate.

I'm not trying to prove anything to you. I'm not trying to prove that I was the father you believed me to be when you were very young. I've made some mistakes but I have no idea what they were. And I've never desired to start over again. I have no desire to eliminate parts of myself. I have no desire. Maybe we should meet as complete strangers and talk deep into the night as though we'd never seen each other before. All we know is that there is something reminiscent, something mysteriously connected. Sometimes.

You put up flags on sticks in order to guide the memory. In order to guide something. In other words, something stands out. A flag on a stick.

Kind of like the Spanish in the 1500s, who staked the plains from the New Mexican border clear up to northern Texas to mark where they'd been and where they were going. Because nobody knew. Little red flags on sticks. It was the home of the Comanche, who always knew exactly where they were but to everyone else everything appeared to be lost.

15

I was relatively healthy. My son was very healthy. You, my son. The one who worked with canaries and stone. I think your grandparents, Jay and Aubra, were living in another garage on the other side of town about then. Jay was healthy but Aubra wasn't so healthy. She had a lot of maladies that seemed to get worse when it rained. Hacking. Sneezing. Occasionally throwing up. The problem with it was—this other garage—was that it was in a flood plain. So when it rained really hard they were up to their necks in water. The linoleum would peel and curl and break out of its aluminum boundaries. But up to that point they were happily going arm in arm to the coffee shop that the woman from Berkeley owned who was having an affair with you. She was married at that time but you didn't care about that. She didn't care about that either. Marriage. You were in love. She had lots of coffee and she was in attendance almost always at her coffee shop. Your grandparents would walk down there arm in arm. They were very much in love too. They had always been. Aubra kept pretending that everything was alright. They would go down there to the coffee shop. They would walk across the zocalo—the little park—in those days it looked like an old Mexican village. They would sit at a corner table looking out at the zocalo through a big picture window and see the migrant workers talking about family problems. For instance, women. They were always talking about women. Wives, girlfriends. They were always talking about women. Meanwhile, inside the coffee shop Jay and Aubra were holding court over Brazilian coffee talking about Nietzsche and Erroll Garner and taking hot baths. They sat at their circular table by the big picture window in the early morning hours because Jay liked to get up at ungodly hours—four in the morning sometimes. Three in the morning sometimes. He was worse than you. Aubra, on the other hand, used to get migraines and sleep all day. She was getting worse and worse. But Jay loved to get up.

It was around about this time that the rains started and it rained and it rained and it rained and it rained and it rained. It wasn't exactly apocalyptic but it flooded the small town. The flood plain. It flooded the second garage where Jay and Aubra were domiciled. It flooded bad enough where they were forced to leave. The Russian River over-flowed its banks. Bridges were uprooted. Dams exploded. The sky weeped.

Around about this time Jay inherited a sum of money from his dead father and this sum of money was enough in those days to purchase a house. So he and Aubra jumped into their white Chevy Nova and drove out to New Mexico because they had heard through a friend that Columbus, New Mexico, was a brilliant new place to be. Now Columbus was the town that Pancho Villa attacked in 1914 or something like that—and is notoriously the first U.S. town that was invaded from the outside in, including Pearl Harbor, of course. But that was hardly even a town. Columbus was the first town where there was a foreign intrusion, let's say. They sent some General Pershing down there but he never even saw Pancho Villa's dust. Pancho Villa swept down on Columbus, New Mexico. Anyway, when Jay and Aubra reached Columbus, it was entirely different from what they had in their imaginations. Whatever that was. There was black plastic blowing from barbed wire. There were dead pigeons in the road.

They made a big U-turn and drove back to Deming, New Mexico. Deming, just south of Truth or Consequences. Deming, home of duck

Sam Shepard

racing. They drove straight to a real estate agent and asked him if he had anything for sale. He said certainly. So they drove out to this place on the corner of Iron Street and somewhere else and they immediately liked it and Jay gave up all his hard-earned inheritance to the real estate guy and all of a sudden they had a house which they hadn't had before. He owned his own house, which is a good thing I suppose. He owned his own house in a little border town called Deming. That's how they got down there. Look up at the sky, Jay said to Aubra. She looked up—Are you interested in all this? About your ancestors? Your grandma and grandpa? About love?

In the meantime, back in the little town, the little Mexican zocalo town of northern California, you, and the woman who owned the coffee shop, your wife now, were living in perfect harmony. Jay and Aubra moved all their stuff from the flooded second garage to Deming, New Mexico, in a U-Haul trailer. An upright piano, many books, many pictures, many stuffed animals, a burl oak table, a broken down sofa, all the stuff they had accumulated, plus Jay's notebooks, photographs, mildewed and dripping. They moved all that stuff down there to Deming and they started to live a life.

16

In this desert I was originally referring to, the painted desert, you walk across Zen-like sculpted gardens full of carefully raked sand and cactus to get to the Clinic. And these sculptured gardens are full of little signs. They look like dominos from a distance. Signs that read Watch Out for Rattle Snakes. Beware of Rattle Snakes. People come from all over the world to get the cure from the Clinic. The magic cure. People drive up in fancy limousines. People are pushed in high tech wheelchairs by well appointed orderlies into the famous clinic. Sliding glass doors part in front of them. On the foyer wall are the pictures of the two brothers who first started the clinic in Minnesota. They're in a snowstorm. They have snowshoes on. Heavy overcoats. They're bringing the cure to the wilderness. Snow is flying everywhere. Outside here in the desert it's 112 degrees but these men trudge in the snow with beatific smiles on their faces. It's a gigantic mural that sweeps from one

Sam Shepard

side of the clinic to the other. Bigger than life size.
You can hear the blizzard winds blowing. But just
outside in Arizona it's 112 degrees and there are
sculptured gardens full of sand and cactus and
rattle snakes. Bigger than life itself.

17

Once upon a time there was a Pancho Villa who came from Durango, Old Mexico, which at that time was the very end of the Santa Fe Trail. Or the beginning of it. Depending on which way you were going. In other words the Santa Fe Trail sort of began around St. Louis, Missouri. If you were American that is. This was in the days when America was very isolated. Surrounded by enemies. The Santa Fe Trail went from Missouri and then all the way down to Durango, Old Mexico, where Pancho Villa was born. And Dolores del Río also was born there. There's a Dolores del Río Boulevard in the middle of Durango. If anybody gives a shit. Anyway, right after the Mexican Revolution Pancho Villa retired to a hacienda just outside Durango. They discovered he was no longer the core of the revolution. There was an Indian in the south called Emiliano Zapata who was more politically important. Pancho Villa was living in this hacienda and having a good time. He had his hacienda and he had a brown Dodge sedan that

was chauffeured and he had many many body-
guards. Villa would periodically go to town to col-
lect gold from the bank in order to pay his many
many peons and people who worked for him at the
hacienda. On one particular day he decided to go
to the bank. And so they took off in the Dodge
sedan and they went to the town of Durango,
Mexico, and they went to the bank and they got
bags of gold in order to pay all the peons. So they
got back in the Dodge and they headed out of the
dusty town back to the hacienda and suddenly a
boy, a young boy nine or ten, jumps out—he was a
pumpkin seed vendor and he was barefooted and
he had a huge sombrero and a sack of seeds over
his shoulder. He came out yelling Pancho Villa's
name. Very excited. He got in front of the Dodge
waving his skinny arms and he said, "Pancho Villa,
Pancho Villa! Hail Pancho Villa!" And that was the
signal for all the assassins to come out of hiding
and shoot Pancho Villa dead in his brown Dodge.
That's the last anybody ever heard of him. "Pancho
Villa, Pancho Villa! Hail Pancho Villa!" That was
the end of that. End of story.

Durango's still there, the desert's still there,
Mexico's still there. Everything's still there but

everything's changed. Jay and Aubra went to New Mexico and they had absolutely nothing to do with Pancho Villa. They were two different subjects, two different entities, that lived not even in the same time.

18

I don't like the idea of him talking about Pancho Villa. Whether he's overheard it or learned it through gossip or comic books he's got things wrong. To me the story of Pancho Villa is completely private and belongs to the world of fable. Why should he be poking his nose into information that's private? It has nothing to do with him, it's not his story to tell.

19

There's some things you don't know about me mainly because they happened before you were born. For some reason they stand out in my memory. Then they didn't, now they do. For instance, you don't know that I used to sleep on a mattress on the floor on the corner of Avenue C and Tenth Street on the Lower East Side, in a condemned building. I used to sleep there on my mattress in a corner of the floor. And I used to heat the whole place with a gas stove, it was a shotgun apartment, floor-through, there was no furniture at all—just stuff found on the street. And one night I was sleeping and I was awakened by a woman screaming. I debated whether to go down and help her, whether to go downstairs and see who it was. All kinds of things were running through my mind. I stared at the blue flame coming from the gas stove in the kitchen. I had a moral dilemma. And finally I got up enough courage to go down there and I went to the bottom stairs and left the building and I saw her trapped by a man who was beating her up. As soon as I appeared they both stopped and turned and looked at me. They had the dumbest blank stares on their faces just like that doctor in the painted desert. And she said, the woman said to my face, "What the hell are you looking at?" I turned around and ran back upstairs and the woman continued to scream from the street. The man continued to beat her.

20

The time that I'm trying to get at—the time I'm trying to get at here is a fragile time. Like a scab very crusty, very small that you pick at. It's somewhat muddied, this time. It's not at all clear to me. It must have been—it must have been, I would say, in the mid-seventies. Thereabouts. What went down? It's not at all clear. Cambodia. Tet Offensive. Helicopters crashing. Watergate. Muhammad Ali. Float like a butterfly sting like a bee. The chestnut king of the Triple Crown leading the Belmont field by thirty-two lengths. Regardless how you thread them there's no escape from the confusion of that time.

21

This period I'm referring to must have been somewhere in the mid-seventies. Wasn't it? Nixon. Somewhere. Somehow. Somewhat. Escaped. I can't talk about the actual escape much except to say that it was exhausting. It was mentally exhausting. It still is. All the planning all the preparation for it and then the experience of course was quite different than the plans. The experience is always different than the plans. The experience was exhausting. I am still exhausted from it. Angel Island. Escape from Alcatraz. Three escaped. Thought they drowned. Maybe only one drowned. A blurry photograph from 1975. Recent computer-generated evidence suggesting two made it to South America, just like Butch Cassidy and the Sundance Kid.

The thing that always fascinated me about Alcatraz was how you could see the whole city from the shore. You could see straight out to the whole cityscape. The Golden Gate, the Oakland Bay. You could see everything. The peaceful city with lights twinkling. The city going on in spite of Alcatraz. So it would seem as though if you were standing on the shoreline of Alcatraz you could easily swim across the bay to the big city. However, the bay itself was very treacherous. There are shifting currents out there. Sometimes they go east to west. Sometimes west to east. Sometimes north to south. Multiple currents. Any which way. In any case, you could get chopped up by a motorboat and there were all kinds of boats out there. Big barges. Ocean liners. Rowboats. Fishing boats. Tugboats. Tourist boats. Chopped up by one of these. Very treacherous. Anyway, I was so exhausted by the chaos of this era that I couldn't even get in the water to dog paddle.

I remember Lee Marvin distinctly getting in the water of Alcatraz and lying on his back as though he were going to backstroke across the bay. Like it was luxurious to him. The water and all its currents was a luxurious thing. It was easy, almost lazy. It was like nobody had ever thought of it. And there he was backstroking across the bay. He lay down backwards in the water. He didn't actually do the backstroke but you had the impression he was going to at any moment. *Point Blank.* 1967 or something like that. And Angie Dickinson tried to beat him up. She tried to beat Lee Marvin up. She pounded furiously on his chest. She slapped him and hacked him and I thought she was doing a pretty good job of it. But he just stood there. It wasn't a test of manhood or strength or anything. He just stood there and she exhausted herself. It was a kind of rope-a-dope contest. He stood there and Angie Dickinson beat on him and then fell to her knees crumpled. A crumpled woman. There she was. And then later in retaliation she turned on all the appliances in the kitchen. The mixer, the toaster, the washing machine, all this stuff, and he had to go around and turn it all off. She taunted him. He taunted her. It was a taunting movie.

What can I say about the escape. Like I said before, there are many plans. There's the lying awake in bed staring at the ceiling, the cement ceiling. Preparing to scrape the plaster with the cafeteria spoon, the metal grate, the tunnel itself, the passage.

The work itself went fairly fast once I got inside the tunnel, other than the usual cobwebs and spiders and things crawling around. At least there's a light at the end of the tunnel. But when I got down there I saw that now the path was vertical rather than horizontal. It was going upwards, so I had to get some rope. I had to find some rope and I actually made it, I made the rope, out of sheets, and found my way upstairs. And when I got upstairs, then, of course, I had to jump. I had to jump quite a distance. I never knew I had it in me. But I jumped up and managed to wedge myself between the rafters and got upstairs and it was a whole different world up there.

I probably shouldn't be telling you all this should I. My escape. Backpedaling across the bay. Now you know Now you know that I am an escaped prisoner. Now you know. Then you didn't. Now you do. You know too much. Somebody's going to have to do away with you. Maybe this character who's been dogging me all this time.

Let me start over. I can start over. You'll allow me to start over please. Like I said I got nothing to prove to you. I'm not trying to be a hero in any-body's eyes. I'm not sure if it was the mid-seventies in fact I think it wasn't the mid-seventies I'm not sure. It wasn't the mid-eighties either. I think it was the mid-nineties. That's a twenty-year dif-ference. Now how is it possible to not remember something for a twenty-year span? Something like that. A whole life. Twenty years is a long time. Some people don't even live twenty years. Some people live a lot less. Some people die the moment they're born. Okay let me start over. There was a time when the whole thing seemed like a fairy tale. Once upon a time—once upon a period in the past. It might have been the nineties, the mid-nineties there was so much going on. It might have been much earlier than that, I don't know. All I know is it was an interim of my life. This fragile time. Many different things going on and so many of those different things seemed to matter. Now they don't. Then they did, but now they don't. Napalm. Cambodia. Nixon. Tet Offensive. Watergate. Secretariat. Muhammad Ali.

22

There are times when I can't help thinking about the past. I know the present is the place to be. It's always been the place to be. I know I've been recommended by very wise people to stay in the present as much as possible, but the past sometimes presents itself. The past doesn't come as a whole. It always comes in parts.

In fact it comes apart. It presents itself as though it was experienced in fragments.

Why? Why, for instance, is the past . . . . . Excuse me . . . . . why, for instance, is the present preferred to the past? Because assumedly the present is what's making memories. It's what's making the past. Sometimes it seems very fleeting.

What exactly is the experience of the present? The experience of the present is one of anonymity. Complete anonymity. The way the sun hits the pavement. The way it hits your bare feet. The way dog shit squeezes between your toes. The way a quarter goes a long way. The way a quarter used to go a long way. The way a quarter could buy you

Sam Shepard

an Abba-Zaba. The way chlorine smells. The way
chlorine attacks your nostrils. The way your trunks
fit. The way water comes over your head. The way
your eyes open underwater and see things. What
do you see? You see other people, other human
beings struggling to keep their eyes open underwater. The present is a many-faceted thing. Much
like the past.

But the present comes with a tangible experience, he says, rocking back and forth. Rocking.
Rocking. He says, pausing. No but wait a second
just a second what about miracles. What about
the cure? There has to be a cure. At one point in
the past—at some point in the past—everything
was alright. There was no desperation. Everything
worked. So what is the cure. Is there some way to
cure the present? Can we do something as simple
as taking a hot bath of mineral water. Or do we
have to start all over. There must be a cure. We
are children of the miraculous. Long pause. Pausing. A long pause. Pausing. Nobody hangs on his
words. Nobody hangs in the moment. Nobody
really hangs for nobody.

23

I have binoculars now so I can just make out through the screen porch that he is sitting and it's not a rocker like I originally thought but it's more of a sliding office chair affair. Some kind with big wheels and adjustable armrests and he slides from one position to another. I don't know what he did with the rocker. Sometimes he slides in circles on his chair like he's floating on air. I don't know, I can't tell, and he's got a small oval table with iced tea and a stack of stuff on it. It looks to be a lot of papers and a fat book. Yes, there is a book. It's open to page 399, that's how good my binoculars are. He stands up vertically to turn every single page. He doesn't just lick his thumb and turn the page, he stands each time. It's an old-fashioned book. *Jane's Fighting Ships 1942*. A big fat thick book probably about 900 pages but he's on page 399. This seems to be his only form of exercise. Standing up and turning the pages.

24

Aubra, your grandmother, whose real name was Aubra Steagle, that's the name she came with, the name she got off the boat with, the name of her first husband, Steagle. That's it. She actually came from a foreign country, she was from England, I think, and she never got green papers or any of the stuff you were supposed to have to make you legal, so she was an illegal immigrant, actually. They were trying to get her name straight, so that she would qualify for some kind of health insurance. What was her maiden name? Her mother's maiden name. There were lots of questions. There were a lot of things wrong with her. She was coming apart. So they had to go down to the city hall in the little western town of Deming. And the city hall had these huge photographs that were now reprinted in a kind of sepia tone. I don't know why, maybe to make them appear older than they actually were. But there were pictures of the pioneer days of Deming back in the 1880s—you know, rows of mules, horses in the muck, carriages, lamplights, the hustle and bustle of a border pioneer town. Anyway, Jay was very persistent about this. He wanted insurance for Aubra and every day they would go down to the little city hall and they would wait in line for this, for her green papers. They went through all this red tape, phone calls and phone calls and phone calls. It was a phone tree in which you stayed on the line and it said if you want such and such person you press 4, if you want such and such another person you press 2, if you want such and such another person you press 12, something like that. And you never found a person at all. Just a disembodied voice. They had to be very careful because this was after 9/11 and the government was suspicious, little towns were suspicious, everybody was suspicious that something was going on. Everybody was paranoid. Particularly of immigrants. So if it was found out that she had no papers, that she had no right to be here in America, land of Lady Liberty, that she would get deported immediately, put on a boat and sent back to jolly old England, where when she was a child the place was getting bombed by the Germans.

25

I'm probably not a paranoid person. I mean paranoid is not the first thing you'd come up with in describing me. But yesterday my sisters left me alone for about five minutes on the porch and I saw a glimpse of something across the street. A glimpse of something silver. I was amazed at how it gleamed in the morning light. I looked and I saw this pair of binoculars that looked like owls' eyes. There was someone in a chair much like me who was putting the binoculars away. He was putting them away in a leather case. But I thought, goodness gracious why would he be looking at me? I don't know anybody in this town. No one has even heard of me. Then here I am being watched by a stranger. It gave me the oddest feeling. As though I'm a wild animal or something. But maybe he's a bird watcher. I've watched birds myself very close up through binoculars. Maybe he's totally innocent and I'm just being paranoid. There are birds around here of all different varieties. Blue jays.

Blackbirds. Sparrows. Towhees. But I've never considered them to be very exotic. Maybe that's all he was doing. Watching birds from a distance. From across the street.

26

Now there are swallows dive-bombing all around the house. I think they are on an insect hunt. There are at least three or four of them. Maybe as many as six. They have a rust and blue color about them. They are very fast. They are like little jets. They just fly around and dive-bomb. You can't even see the insects they are after. They could be imaginary insects, but they're not.

There are so many of them, in fact, the air is full of insects, we just can't see them. It's a hot, clear day, a slight breeze. There's the occasional mockingbird that comes down and lands and sings his song. A song that he's imitated. A song he's picked up. They are uncanny little birds. I used to awaken to mockingbirds. I used to go to sleep with mockingbirds. They were all singing songs they made up. From the light posts at night. A whimsical little bird. Any time of day. They have a kind of melancholy. For me they have a kind of melancholy, but it's not sad, it's just typical. A bird that is typical of a place, that's all. A place in time.

ter emerged from the darkness of the house. He asked her to sit down beside him. She pulled up a wrought iron garden chair and wiped the raindrops off the seat. She sat down as though she were in school listening attentively, leaning toward him.

He said the room in his mind was an extension of a garage. It was a garage unlike any he'd seen since then. In his mind it had windows all around about five feet off the ground. Narrow windows.

—Wait a minute, Dad, what room? What are you talking about?

—The room with the narrow windows. They looked out at an old racetrack.

—Which racetrack? Where was it?

There were cars parked on the backstretch. There was a chain link fence running along the turf course, which was downhill intersecting the main track. From the hill at the top of the chain link fence everything was very still, very quiet. It wasn't until the horses had gone almost six furlongs before you heard the crowd and then you heard them stamping and screaming, caterwauling, making all kinds of sounds. From that point the horses were about the size of pencil sharpeners. They started out regular size and then they became very small. A shot rang out. A single shot. From some kind of carbine or rifle with a scope. Immediately the crowd went silent. Immediately you saw the line of horses swerve around the leader who was down on the ground with the jockey squirming. Legs flailing in the air, jockey silks ripped asunder. The saddle stripped of all its color. The bridle broken in half in the horse's mouth. Pundits were jumping the fence. All kinds of backstretch help. Grooms. Handlers. Exercise boys, exercise girls, running in all directions, screaming and pointing. The rest of the field crossed the line. Now the crowd started to yell. A siren was heard in the distance. Bells were ringing but not in jubilation. Emergency bells. Everything was in a state of emergency.

She leaned closer. When was this, Dad? I don't remember anything like this.

The man who fired the carbine, who fired the gun with the scope, who brought the lead horse down, was discovered sitting cross-legged in a cargo van. He said that he was assigned to be an assassin. He got his orders from Mount Rushmore.

He was fleeing the scene of the crime. He jumped down, threw the gun in a sage bush and ran for his life. He ran til he came to a Gulf station, where he asked for ice. The owner was glad to give it to him. He sat down with two fresh bags of ice and began crunching them while the owner called the police. He asked the owner if there was a room. There's got to be a room in this town. The owner shrugged. He said there might be one. There's a slim chance. The man asked how much the room was. "Ten dollars," the owner said.

"I'll take it," replied the man. "I'll take it."

After that I left the state. I left and I never came back until now. And now I want to find out where that room was. Now it seems important. Then it didn't, now it does. The color of the jockey's silks. The color of the horses. The bookies all in a line. The morning odds. The coffee and black beans. The priests running for cover. The greyhounds barking at rag dolls. This ten-dollar-a-day room.

The wind is whipping the walnuts now. Little green balls. They're all swirling, everything is swirling. The peach trees are swirling, the crepe myrtles are swirling, the magnolias are swirling. The sky has turned a steely gray. The whole sky has turned. We are going to get a storm.

—I probably shouldn't have told you all that. But then again you weren't born yet.

—It's okay, Dad. You can tell me anything. But I think we should go inside now. It's going to rain.

—Can you take me to the grocery store? he says

to her suddenly. Could you take me down there in this wheelchair now? Could you buy me some stuff? I'll need a few things. I'll need some mayonnaise and a silver tin of sardines, a banana. I'll need some buckwheat flapjack mix. I might need some instant coffee. Could you take me there and see what they've got?

I'm following right behind them in the half-light, it begins to drizzle. The wind is kicking the dust up. She hesitates. He says to her, Keep going.

Where is he going now? Where does he think he's going? Is he leaving this town forever? Will I ever see him again?

She pushes the wheelchair straight ahead. She says to him above his head, the mounting wind, both facing the same direction.

—Dad? Dad? Why do you need these things now? Why all these supplies? You're not going hunting.

—No, I'm not going hunting. At least I'm not hunting for food. Just keep going.

—Besides, I don't know where this room might be, this garage. I have no idea, especially if it's all in your head.

—All in my head? he says to her, as they go bumping along as the rain starts pelting the narrow road. Everything's in my head.

28

You notice the progressive nature of things. Things run down. You notice how different. You don't want to believe it. You notice for instance his breathing, the lack of breath. You notice for instance the reach of his arms, the lack of coordination between his brain and his hands. Who is it this time? For instance, if the head . . . For instance, if the neck is allowed to rest back and be aligned with the spine on a fairly even level and the head is allowed to rest back against the Adirondack chair then the air that is going in and out the passage of the neck is allowed to move. When that happens the brain and the mind tend to think a little more freely.

What happens if the head rocks forward and causes the neck to double over creating a kind of stoppage, where not only is the breathing interrupted but the thought as well? The thought and the brain don't operate at the same level as they do when the throat is open.

For instance, when the eyes are closed and the

sounds are allowed to come in, where the sounds are more pronounced. For instance, the distant highway. The sound of the jays, which always reminds me of the Rocky Mountains and high altitude. Sounds of red-winged blackbirds, chicka-dees. Sounds of wrens, crickets, butterfly wings. But what happens if you cut that off completely? No sound at all. No thinking. No thought. What happens if it ends right there?

29

J ay was going up and down the highway, with Aubra in his white Chevy Nova. He was going from clinic to clinic. All the way to Arizona and back. He was trying to find a doctor to make her better. He was trying to get her healthy. Everything was going wrong with her. Her luxurious red hair was falling out. Her green eyes were going blind. She had an aluminum wheelchair. She was getting weaker and weaker. Jay was working all day in the deli and she was getting weaker and weaker. There were transfusions. There was a brain hemorrhage. There were swollen veins. There were oxygen tanks. There were bandages. There were tubes. There was breathing. Heavy breathing.

Jay was having a hard time of it. Going up and down the road looking for a cure to what really ailed Aubra. He was desperate. He tried everything, dialysis, he tried it all. And she wasn't getting any better. She was losing a lot of blood. A lot of weight.

He was in a doctor's office and she was almost going unconscious. And coming back. Going away. Coming back. Going away. Coming back. And he said to the doctor, he said to the doctor, "What's wrong with her?" And the doctor simply turned to him and he said, "She's dying."

Jay was in the Mexican deli sorting bottles of ketchup and hot sauce, lining them up behind the mayonnaise. The Muzak was on. Somebody asked him who he liked better, the Green Bay Packers or the Pittsburgh Steelers. The phone rang, somebody told him his wife was in trouble. He took off his apron and ran out into the parking lot. When he got to his house the police were already there. The neighbors were standing around in the yard. He ran into the house. The police wanted to know his name. They wanted to know Aubra's name. She was dead but they wanted to know her name. They wanted to know what kind of pills she was taking. They wanted to know the names of the pills. How long she'd been taking them. He could see her lying dead in the bed from the corner of his eye. They asked him if he wanted to be alone with her. He said no. It was already too late. He left the room, passing neighbors who were offering condolences. A white truck pulled up and two huge men got out and went into the house. They carried Aubra's body in a black bag back to the truck. They drove off. The police went away. The neighbors went back to their houses. A cat ran across the yard.

30

Chicano gangs in lime-green jumpsuits. Low-riders in purple Mercurys. Pregnant girls barely fifteen. Priests in black robes. Choirs singing Catholic prayers. Church bells are ringing twelve noon as Jay walks back to work at the deli. They ask him who he likes better, Green Bay or the Pittsburgh Steelers. They ask him how old he is. Where he's from. Back east, he says. Back east.

Jay returns home. He's walking slightly slumped forward. He carries a big sack of cat food on his back from the deli. There are wild feral cats all over the neighborhood, some of them are babies. He shakes the cat food out on the curb in front of his house. He goes back into his house, crumbling up the empty bag. He closes the door and drags a chair in front of the window. He looks out and sees the cats coming from all directions. They start eating the cat food but they always keep one eye on guard. From across the street Jay sees two gray dogs, they come directly toward the cats. The cats keep eating. The dogs keep coming. Jay stands up inside the house. The cats jump. The dogs pounce. Everything is scattered.

Iron Street. The sky a brilliant golden sunset. Real golden. Beyond what the Spanish conceived. Really golden skies.

Now in the zocalo in the little lost town, of northern California, where the migrant workers wait on corners, hiding from soldiers in dark costumes. Soldiers sneaking around through the bushes. Making sure the president's name is not spoken in vain. Making sure there are no whispered plans to overthrow the real estate. To overthrow the banks. Listening intently to the Spanish verbs that are being spoken by the immigrant men on the corner. Forgetting how to conjugate. Wished they had finished elementary school.

What is a green card exactly? It allows the holder to work? It allows the holder citizenship? It allows the holder to travel freely? Does the possession of a green card mean you don't have to climb a wall? You don't have to dig a tunnel? You don't have to worry about where your mother was born? Where your father was born? Do we understand the men talking in a foreign language on the corner? Do we try to understand where they might have come from? Maybe the wind blew them in.

There are trucks loaded with masked men looking for immigrants of all kinds. Looking for enemies of the people behind coffee shops. Behind
shoe stores. Behind wineries. They call their
bosses. They tell their bosses that here in the little
zocalo of this little town everything is quiet and
peaceful.

32

I don't know how he stands the monotony, to tell you the truth. Hiding in the bushes day after day after day after day after day after day after day the same thing over and over again. Although internally something must change, externally it remains fairly constant. Maybe we could become friends. Maybe if I sat here long enough he would come up behind me. I don't have to see his face. I'm hollow back there anyway. Kind of like a shell. Like a milk chocolate egg that's hollow inside. Maybe we can strike up a conversation. He must be waiting too. We're both waiting. Maybe he has something to say that would clear things up for both of us. For instance, was he hired by some big company? Was he hired by the government? Or is he just plain nosy. Why does he care about my monotony? It's not my monotony anyway. It's his, too. It's both of ours. It's everybody else's. I mean it's about ninety degrees. There's white butterflies on purple flowers. There's bugs buzzing over the green cut lawn. There's flowers coming out on the magnolias. There's marigolds, there's tomatoes. Lots of tomatoes. But what is it? Why doesn't he say something? Even if it's about the weather. Why doesn't he talk to me? I'm a likable person. The same the same the same over and over again.

What is it about it that drags you down, that makes you feel as though you're never going to overcome, you're never going to overcome something. I don't know what it is. Monotony. Sameness. It must be the same for him. I don't know why he haunts me day after day. He stares at the bugs going across the top of the cut grass, the mowed grass, and every once in a while alighting on a lawn chair. What is it? What could possibly fascinate him about that? About me? Maybe he's not fascinated. Maybe he is the opposite of fascinated. What would the opposite of fascinated be? To be tangled up in thought, in thinking. Tangled up. There he is looking at the same thing day after day, month after month. Butterflies landing on purple plants.

33

Sometimes he does this thing where he shakes his head violently from side to side as though a bug of some kind is bugging him as though the bug is trying to get in his nostrils but it's not a bug at all it's the hair on his face or the imagined hair on his face or him trying to prevent the imagined hair getting on his face. He shakes his head and one of his sisters stands and combs his hair with a brush, a brush with tiny plastic teeth. She also uses hairspray, women's hairspray, to keep the hair back. The imagined hair. He always closes his nose or tries to close his nose because evidently the spray is perfumed and he's trying not to smell it. He also has this one gesture that is very curious where he rocks back and forth. He rocks and he'll clasp both hands together like he's praying and he'll brace his arms from the elbow to the wrist. He'll brace both elbows against his stomach and then he'll raise both hands to his face using the left knee in this jerky sort of fashion where the leg is actually propelling the arms toward his face and then he simply itches his upper lip or his left nostril or something like that because evidently the nostrils are trying to tell him something. They're trying to tell him that things have changed.

Both eyebrows! Both eyebrows. Both. No, no just the left. The left. Yes! That's it. Oh good, that's it. Thank God that's it. Thanks. Thanks for that. Things have changed again. Things have changed. Now he has to ask other people. Now he can't do without other people. Things have really changed.

Can you imagine, for instance, something crawling up your ear? It's easy to imagine something like that. Crawling up your ear. And pretty soon you have an itch. It's easy to imagine something like that. Crawling through your hair. Is something crawling through my hair? Is there an ant, for instance. Is there a worm? Is there a fly? An insect of some kind, winged? Mosquito? A leggy insect. An insect with many tentacles that is searching around through my hair for something imagined? You imagine and then you go on to imagine the itch and pretty soon you have one. You have an itch. And pretty soon you ask for help.

34

The driver opens the limousine door. Sandaled feet emerge from the bottom of the flowing blue tunic. He approaches the clinic with his aluminum walker. He's been looking forward to this moment ever since he was diagnosed. He crosses the sands of the sculpted gardens. A green Mojave rattlesnake appears from nowhere and pierces his ankle. He goes down. He is wallowing in the sand like a wounded burro. The driver doesn't know what to do. Nurses come running from the clinic. Everyone is bewildered. Help! he says, and as he loses consciousness he glimpses the image of two brothers in snowshoes who started the most famous clinic in the world.

35

I've all kinds of sensations now. Sensations I've never had before. For instance, I want to see if there's a real estate agent who will cooperate with me. Who will cooperate with me getting the house next door to his. Whether that house is for sale or not. I must get that house and move in. I must contact my tax woman. I must contact my bookie. I need to procure all my earnings. I must have that house. I must be able to see in the windows. I must see whether or not he puts himself to bed at night. Whether or not he gets himself up in the morn-ing. Whether or not he says his prayers. Whether or not he uses the Lord's name. Whether or not he believes in an afterlife. Whether or not he says prayers over meals. Whether or not he helps with the dishes. I must have 24-hour-a-day surveillance. Is there some interlude, or does he go right for the newspaper? Does he read the headlines? Does someone read the headlines to him? I must find out where he comes from. Where he is going to. And what he hopes to accomplish. I must find out the reason behind the blue sign. The blue handicapped sign in his white car. Did he have it manufactured somehow? Did he have it counterfeited? Is there anything really wrong with him? Is he faking? If he's faking should I call him on it? Should I walk right up on his front porch and rap on the front door? Should I present him with my credentials? Should I go for the throat? Or should I just let everything go the way it's going.

36

One year ago he could hear the walnuts drop. He could hear the walnuts crunch. He could scratch the belly of his Catahoula who had too many puppies. Who his youngest son, his skinny boy, insisted on keeping.

One year ago exactly he could drive across the great divide. He could drive down the coastline. The rugged coast. He could yawn at the desert.

One year ago exactly more or less, he could walk with his head up. He could see through the air. He could wipe his own ass.

37

Full moon. East Water Street, the same little town from long ago late at night, well it wasn't late at night when we left, it was relatively early and the moon hadn't risen yet. I'd say it was 6:30 or 7. I was in a wheelchair with a shaggy sheepskin covering the seat and a Navajo blanket over my knees, and my two sons, two of my sons, Jesse and Walker, were on either side pushing me down the middle of East Water Street. I'll never forget the strength I felt from my two boys behind me. Following us were my daughter Hannah, her two friends, both of my sisters and my daughter-in-law, nine of us altogether and we turned right by a three-story church that was all clapboard and there was a huge pine tree in the front and it was already getting dark.

Dusk, dark dusk. The moon was slowly beginning to rise. And we got to a Mexican place called El Farolito and they pushed me boldly in the wheelchair from the quiet street through two swinging doors into the reverberations of an enormous room. A rising cacophony of voices, conversations on top of conversations raucous laughter glasses shattering clinking silverware people shouting to be heard.

We maneuvered through the crowd to the bar at the back of the restaurant. Polished steel, highly polished steel. A mural of rows and rows of blue agave cactus. Cultivated to make tequila and mescal. Brushstrokes and there was all this tequila lined up on long narrow silver shelves bolted to the wall. Hornitos, Cabo Wabo, Sauza, Patrón, Cuervo, Herradura. All different kinds of tequila. They ordered margaritas. My daughter Hannah, her friends Molly and Chad and Jesse's wife, Maura, my sisters Roxanne and Sandy, a whole lot of people at the table and my wheelchair took up two spaces almost. That's how wide it was and I ordered a beef enchilada and a Cabo Wabo. The menu had a logo of a lighthouse. Lonely illuminated. I can't remember exactly what we talked about. Probably Trump, the country in a Mexican standoff, the dogs, the Catahoula, maybe fishing, the usual. The point is a lot of conversation, a lot of people talking at once, the whole table bustling with conversation. Now we were part of them. The bar sounded like a marimba band without the music. A lot of noise and a lot more tequila.

Our whole troupe, our little band, hit the street. The thing I remember most is being more or less helpless and the strength of my sons. A man pushed by his sons in a wheelchair from a crowded restaurant to a street with nobody on it. A man sitting on shaggy wool with a Navajo blanket across his knees.

The moon is getting bigger and brighter. The Strawberry Moon. Spotlighting our little troupe. The full moon. Two sons and their father, everyone trailing behind. Going up the middle of East Water Street and it's really bright now. The full moon. We made it and we hobbled up the stairs. Or I hobbled. My sons didn't hobble, I hobbled.

Sam Shepard began working on *Spy of the First Person* in 2016. His first drafts were written by hand, as he was no longer able to use a typewriter due to complications of ALS. When handwriting became impossible, he recorded segments of the book, which were then transcribed by his family. He dictated the remaining pages when recording became too difficult. Sam's longtime friend Patti Smith assisted him in editing the manuscript. He reviewed the book with his family and dictated his final edits a few days before he passed away on July 27, 2017.

Acknowledgments

Hannah, Walker, and Jesse would like to thank Sam's sisters, Roxanne and Sandy, for their love and care of our father and their invaluable help in bringing this book about.

A Note About the Author

Sam Shepard was the Pulitzer Prize–winning author of more than fifty-five plays and three story collections. As an actor, he appeared in more than sixty films, and received an Oscar nomination in 1984 for *The Right Stuff*. He was a finalist for the W. H. Smith Literary Award for his story collection *Great Dream of Heaven*. In 2012 he was awarded an honorary doctorate from Trinity College, Dublin. He was a member of the American Academy of Arts and Letters, received the Gold Medal for Drama from the Academy, and was inducted into the Theater Hall of Fame. He died in 2017.